Dinosaurios y animales prehistóricos/Dinosaurs and Prehistoric Animals

Diplodocus/Diplodocus

por/by Janet Riehecky

Traducción/Translation: Dr. Martín Luis Guzmán Ferrer
Editor Consultor/Consulting Editor: Dra. Gail Saunders-Smith

Consultor/Consultant: Jack Horner, Curator of Paleontology
Museum of the Rockies
Bozeman, Montana

Mankato, Minnesota

Pebble Plus is published by Capstone Press,
151 Good Counsel Drive, P.O. Box 669, Mankato, Minnesota 56002.
www.capstonepress.com

Copyright © 2007 by Capstone Press. All rights reserved.
No part of this publication may be reproduced in whole or in part, or stored in a retrieval system, or transmitted in any form or by any means, electronic, mechanical, photocopying, recording, or otherwise, without written permission of the publisher. For information regarding permission, write to Capstone Press, 151 Good Counsel Drive, P.O. Box 669, Dept. R, Mankato, Minnesota 56002.
Printed in the United States of America

1 2 3 4 5 6 12 11 10 09 08 07

Library of Congress Cataloging-in-Publication Data
Riehecky, Janet, 1953–
    [Diplodocus. Spanish & English]
    Diplodocus = Diplodocus/por Janet Riehecky.
    p. cm. —(Pebble Plus. Dinosaurios y animales prehistóricos)
    Includes index.
    ISBN-13: 978-0-7368-7637-7 (hardcover : alk. paper)
    ISBN-10: 0-7368-7637-5 (hardcover : alk. paper)
    ISBN-13: 978-0-7368-9935-2 (softcover pbk.)
    ISBN-10: 0-7368-9935-9 (softcover pbk.)
    1. Diplodocus—Juvenile literature. I. Title. II. Title: Diplodocus.
QE862.S3R535618 2007
567.913—dc22   2006027785

Summary: Simple text and illustrations present diplodocus, their body parts, and behavior—in both
    English and Spanish.

Editorial Credits
Sarah L. Schuette, editor; Katy Kudela, bilingual editor; Eida del Risco, Spanish copy editor;
    Linda Clavel, set designer; Wanda Winch, photo researcher

Illustration and Photo Credits
Jon Hughes, illustrator
Thomas R. Wilcox, 21

The author dedicates this book to her niece Sarah.

Note to Parents and Teachers

The Dinosaurios y animales prehistóricos/Dinosaurs and Prehistoric Animals set supports national science standards related to the evolution of life. This book describes and illustrates diplodocus in both English and Spanish. The images support early readers in understanding the text. The repetition of words and phrases helps early readers learn new words. This book also introduces early readers to subject-specific vocabulary words, which are defined in the Glossary section. Early readers may need assistance to read some words and to use the Table of Contents, Glossary, Internet Sites, and Index sections of the book.

Table of Contents

A Spiky Dinosaur 4
How Diplodocus Looked 8
What Diplodocus Did 16
The End of Diplodocus 20
Glossary 22
Internet Sites 24
Index 24

Tabla de contenidos

Un dinosaurio con púas 4
Cómo eran los diplodocus 8
Qué hacían los diplodocus 16
El fin del diplodocus 20
Glosario 23
Sitios de Internet 24
Índice 24

A Spiky Dinosaur

Diplodocus had a long neck and a long tail.

It had spikes on its back.

Un dinosaurio con púas

El diplodocus tenía un cuello largo y una cola larga.

En la espalda tenía púas.

Diplodocus lived
in prehistoric times.
It lived in western
North America about
150 million years ago.

El diplodocus vivió en tiempos
prehistóricos. Vivió hace cerca
de 150 millones de años en
América del Norte.

How Diplodocus Looked

Diplodocus was as long as three fire trucks.

It was about 90 feet (27 meters) long.

Cómo eran los diplodocus

Los diplodocus eran tan largos como tres camiones de bomberos.

Medían cerca de 27 metros (90 pies) de largo.

Diplodocus had
four thick legs.
Diplodocus was so big
that it walked very slowly.

Los diplodocus tenían cuatro
patas gruesas. El diplodocus
era tan grande que tenía
que caminar muy despacio.

Diplodocus had
a very long tail.
Its tail looked like a whip.

El diplodocus tenía una
cola muy larga. Su cola
parecía un látigo.

Diplodocus had short teeth
shaped like pegs.
It stripped leaves from plants
that grew close to the ground.

El diplodocus tenía dientes cortos
en forma de clavija. Con los dientes
arrancaba las hojas de las plantas
que crecían cerca del suelo.

What Diplodocus Did

Female diplodocuses

laid their eggs

while they walked.

The eggs landed safely

on the ground.

Qué hacían los diplodocus

El diplodocus hembra ponía

huevos mientras caminaba.

Los huevos caían en el

suelo sin lastimarse.

Diplodocuses traveled in groups.
They protected their young from other dinosaurs.

Los diplodocus vivían en grupos. Protegían a sus crías de otros dinosaurios.

The End of Diplodocus

Diplodocuses died about 145 million years ago. No one knows why they all died. You can see diplodocus fossils in museums.

El fin del diplodocus

Los diplodocus desaparecieron hace cerca de 145 millones de años. Nadie sabe por qué todos murieron. Tú puedes ver fósiles de diplodocus en los museos.

Glossary

dinosaur—a large reptile that lived on land in prehistoric times

fossil—the remains or traces of an animal or a plant

museum—a place where objects of art, history, or science are shown

prehistoric—very, very old; prehistoric means belonging to a time before history was written down.

protect—to keep safe

whip—a long, thin piece of leather

Glosario

el dinosaurio—reptil grande que vivía sobre la tierra en tiempos prehistóricos

el fósil—restos o vestigios de un animal o una planta

el látigo—pedazo de piel alargado y delgado

el museo—lugar donde se exhiben objetos de arte, historia o ciencias

prehistórico—muy, muy viejo; prehistórico quiere decir perteneciente a una época antes de que hubiera historia escrita.

proteger—evitar el peligro

Internet Sites

FactHound offers a safe, fun way to find Internet sites related to this book. All of the sites on FactHound have been researched by our staff.

Here's how:

1. Visit www.facthound.com

2. Choose your grade level.

3. Type in this book ID **0736876375** for age-appropriate sites. You may also browse subjects by clicking on letters, or by clicking on pictures and words.

4. Click on the **Fetch It** button.

FactHound will fetch the best sites for you!

Index

back, 4
died, 20
eggs, 16
female, 16
food, 14
fossils, 20
groups, 18
legs, 10
lived, 6
museums, 20
neck, 4
North America, 6
prehistoric, 6
size, 4, 8, 10
spikes, 4
tail, 4, 12
teeth, 14
young, 18

Sitios de Internet

FactHound proporciona una manera divertida y segura de encontrar sitios de Internet relacionados con este libro. Nuestro personal ha investigado todos los sitios de FactHound. Es posible que los sitios no estén en español.

Se hace así:

1. Visita www.facthound.com

2. Elige tu grado escolar.

3. Introduce este código especial **0736876375** para ver sitios apropiados según tu edad, o usa una palabra relacionada con este libro para hacer una búsqueda general.

4. Haz clic en el botón **Fetch It**.

¡FactHound buscará los mejores sitios para ti!

Índice

América del Norte, 6
cola, 4, 12
comida, 14
crías, 18
cuello, 4
dientes, 14
espalda, 4
fósiles, 20
grupos, 18
hembra, 16
huevos, 16
murieron, 20
museos, 20
patas, 10
prehistóricos, 6
púas, 4
tamaño, 4, 8, 10
vivió, 6